Thinking Nasty Thoughts

Jesse Chapa Jones

♡ Jesse

ISBN: 1-4774-7638-5
ISBN-13: 9781477476383

Dedication

For my brother, who followed his heart, made his dreams happen – and always believed in me.

Chapter One: *Jeremy*

I have been angry all my life.

There isn't much holding back the rage now that Amy's gone. The rage is going to come out. I feel it like oil sizzling in my blood, the flame at its hottest, the rubber band at its tightest, tidal wave bursting, covering me: red, viscous, dangerous. At stoplights, I fight the urge to ram my truck into whatever's in front of me just to hear the crunch. In the garage, I try not to destroy my own tool bench. The anger crawls, making my neck twitch and my jaw tighten and my breath come quicker, sounding as sharp and round and strong as a bull stamping in the ring. I want excuses to tell someone off, to scream, to slam my fist through a wall, to let it all out in a wild dance with this thing inside me, to fuck something, to fuck something up.

My wife was my buffer, the safety to my trigger. Amy soothed my savage beast, you could say. That old chestnut. When she was around, the rage was merely a soft, radiant heat, like that of stones warmed by an easy afternoon sun. She was the most precious thing in the world.

My ex-wife.

The dark anger was a secret I held close to me always. It made me laugh to myself. I could always use my reserve, if necessary. In my back pocket like a killer jailhouse shank made from a toothbrush. You wouldn't have known it, maybe, looking at me. Yeah, I looked like an average guy, I think. Big dude, you know – good-looking and all – but my strength was generally underestimated.

Never needed it until now.

The waitress wore a sky-blue dress. I squinted to see her, a faded angel against the snow's glare. She had blonde hair with dark roots and fine smile lines which somehow complemented her blue eyes. Her nail polish was hot pink. It looked like Amy's favorite polish: Hollywood Woman. Amy, coyly propped in the doorway in a pink lace teddy, all her parts on display through the scanty material, breasts like firm oranges and the triangle of her sex dark, one hand on her hip. She bit her lip in a way that was innocently sexy. She might as well have been naked. The teddy was better than nakedness, though: something I could tear off with my hands. Like a gift. Hollywood Woman on her toes. Lying in wait for me to come home from work. She never usually did stuff like that, so I *must* have done something right. I took her right there up against the wall, hard, her legs wrapped around my waist.

When I penetrated her, she moaned my name with an intensity that stunned me. *She wanted me to be a man like this.* A man filling her pussy with his cock like there was no tomorrow.

Heavy metal guitars are thrumming ripping sawing in my head. *Is that the bass pounding along or is it my heart?* I tap my spoon against the table in jagged syncope with my mind. A man at the next booth glares at me over his glasses, over his newspaper. I am Disturbing the Peace. I am Acting Inappropriately. I am Evil and Must Be Destroyed. *Can he see smoke rising from my nostrils?* I put my hand to my nose.

Hello. Hello? Fire, police, ambulance. What is your emergency, please?

Oh, shit oh fuck. I see it. THERE IT IS AGAIN!

Outside, in the parking lot. The ostrich. I shake my head like a dog, trying to clear the image. This motherfucker has been *following me.* Tall, velvety dove-gray feathers, one bright eye peering into me – into my core, my soul, into that I wish to hide. The animal is extraordinarily beautiful and…inviolate. The word *inviolate* pleases me, the way it just pops into my mind out of nowhere. I didn't know I knew it, even. I think it means pure.

Hey, I'm smart. What did you think, just because I'm angry and fucked up I'm stupid? I fucking read. I didn't finish college but I fucking read. I have read a lot.

Where did an ostrich even come from around here? Maybe it's a figment of my imagination or even some kind of sign from God. All I know is whenever it appears, it makes my head spin. Proof my grip on reality is going.

Another time. Amy. She was pissed at me because I hadn't finished something unimportant around the house. One of my usual chores: firewood, cleaning gutters, snow shoveling. She was looking for any excuse, prowling through the house, straightening couch cushions and wiping at dust as she fussed tirelessly, a stream of one-sided, mindless conversation. Stressed from work, yada yada. I knew the drill and complied. We fought over dinner, fought doing dishes, fought trying to relax in front of the TV with glasses of wine. She wore a holey white t-shirt with no bra and old maroon sweatpants with her college logo. The more she yelled, the more rigid my cock became. I wanted to release her from her mood, to fuck her into submission, to shut her up with my dick in her mouth. Just wanted to pound her, fill her, feel the way her pussy clutched. Her nipples, dark red through the white fabric, her breath thick with upset, tight emotions I found hard to take. I wondered if this yelling was getting her wet like it was getting me hard.

My wife's livid mouth was stained with wine, slick with lip gloss.

I had enough. Grabbed the back of her head and forced my tongue into that mouth. Amy pushed at me for a minute, her hands against my chest and her *no* against my lips but then she was kissing me back shamelessly, rabidly, smothering me with her tongue in a long kiss, climbing on top of me on the couch, slapping me in the face once, twice – hot damn! – unzipping me, scoring me with her fingernails. We fucked for hours, in every position we could think of and in the morning, I left her tied to the bed when I went to work the early shift, barely able to walk.

God, she'd loved it.

The ostrich is gone.

"More coffee?" the waitress said, motioning with the coffeepot.

I said yes. I took a sip of the coffee. I stared at her mouth.

"Hot," I said. My zipper was straining pleasantly under the table.

"Just brewed it," the waitress said, with a friendly afternoon smile.

"I meant your ass." She stopped smiling and walked away.

Never needed it until now. But now, see, there's nothing left to lose.

I'm gone.

Chapter Two: *Cherry*

Same town, another table.

Cherry was sweet, like her name. Cherry: short for Cherise. Cherry: crisp white button-up shirt, black pinstripe suit, shiny black 2-inch heels. Not too short, not too high. Just right. She worked at a bank and wanted to look good, but not distractingly so. She was sexy. She wore glasses. She went to church. She didn't miss the details. She was a catch.

Cherry ran impatient fingers through strawberry-blonde curls, screwed her lips up at her friend Becca, sipped her gin and tonic. Becca worked part-time at the university library and wrote erotic stories under an assumed name. She wore a dark-green wrap dress, had a mane of wild black hair in a messy ponytail and many visible tattoos. One that covered her whole arm – a sleeve, she called it – had hummingbirds and ivy and purple flames and the words VEGAN POWER. The words lasted longer than the vegan phase. Becca was, in her own words, back to beef.

Becca had broken up with Terence. Again. Terence was a handsome idiot who'd pull a disappearing act whenever things felt serious. And then Becca and Cherry would get together for the emotional debrief at The Tornado, a fusion-cuisine restaurant that was cutting edge. A few years ago, that is. Now it was slightly worn around the edges.

Around them swirled Friday night buzz – men and women murmuring in conversation, small red lamps over the tables giving a furtive devilish glow to the proceedings. Outside, snowflakes and head-lights.

Becca was on her third drink, a feminine rose-colored concoction in a martini glass. "Cher, taste this, it's like strawberry and mango and lovely vodka and some basil leaves or mint or some shit. All refined and shit. This is *how I roll.*" She finished with a swallow.

"Have some more bread to soak that up, why don't you," Cherry said. Ever watchful.

"He was in California on that fucking business trip and *he said he'd call* after the big presentation. He promised. 11pm, he said."

Cherry said, "And he didn't?"

"Hell, no."

"What was going on before California?"

Becca pushed a bite of bread dipped in olive oil into her mouth and talked as she chewed, only leaking a few crumbs. "We were spending a couple nights a week together. I had met some of his friends. He met mine. You know." She swallowed and shrugged, picking up her wineglass. "Everything seemed great. Then he says he felt like California would be good for him because he missed having time to himself."

"To himself? With a bunch of colleagues?"

"I know! That blonde bitch from Finance. The one with the big eyes. I bet he spent some *quality time* with her." Becca threw her hand out in a dismissive wave and knocked her pretty drink on the floor. It splashed on Cherry's boots and the shards of glass tinkled musically. "Oh, *shit*," Becca said, frowning, forlorn and guilty as a little girl.

"Honey, let's get out of here," Cherry said, taking Becca's hand and squeezing it. Becca's eyes looked moist.

"*You* can't understand. *You* have Randy. Best man in the world." Tipsy, Becca was having a hard time putting her arm into her red coat. Cherry jumped up and helped her and Becca said, "Oh, you're my SHE-ro!"

Cherry sighed because she did have Randy. Maybe because she felt he was too pure for her. He made her feel like sin waiting to happen.

She sighed because *she* was still waiting to happen.

"Mark my words," Becca slurred, pointing emphatically at Cherry. "That soul-patched urbane metrosexual is madly in love with you, girl." She burped. "What I wouldn't give for that."

Cherry pulled on a lock of her hair and sighed again, leaning against the table.

"Was Terence, um, good in bed?" she asked.

❧❧

The snow in Boston was not enough to make the bus ride from Logan Airport pretty by any means, but it was enough to distinguish the landscape from Charlotte, where she'd been on a short business trip. This was not the Boston of the Ivy League, but rather a dowdy urban clutter that brought Cherry down and got her thinking of crisp mountain air, or maybe the tang of the coast. Somewhere spacious and unspoiled. She shifted in her seat. The bare trees were traced beautifully in gray pencil against the blue sky; but then there were the rotaries, maddening to navigate by car and littered with gas stations and seafood restaurants and $4.99 Wacky Wednesday Specials and Dunkin Donuts and pawnshops and car dealerships and even a strip club called the Golden Banana, announced on a shit-brown sign with yellow letters.

She sighed and then chuckled to herself, cozying into the bus seat, sipping her coffee. Randy's last *message* on Sunday had been *Held Captive by Temptation.* His talks were called *messages* because *sermon* was too old-school for his church members, mostly in their twenties. Cherry always sat to the front left of the auditorium, admiring Randy as he gracefully commanded the stage, pounding his fist into his hand for effect, or making swooping physical gestures that thrilled. He was handsome, with dark brown hair and blue eyes, medium tall with a body fit from Pilates. And yes, he did have a soul patch, a single small triangle under his lip.

"Temptation," he said into the microphone, pointing his finger forward and peering head-on into the crowd as if to expose his flock. Cherry knew he couldn't see her in the huge auditorium among maybe five hundred others, but just in case she'd worn the yellow v-neck sweater he loved so much. He said it made her look like the sun itself. It made her breasts look amazing. That much she knew.

"Temptation can make you blind. It can definitely test your faith. Am I right?" A murmur, some nervous laughter, rippled the crowd. "Ask yourself. Be honest. Are you using sex, or drugs, or shopping, or alcohol, or yoga, or any other addiction as a *substitute for God?*"

Cherry saw people squirming in their seats. A collective sigh of relief (*or was it just hers?*) escaped when the message finally ended and Randy brought the house band up. No organs or hymns here, but young guys with electric guitars, a wailing girl singer with dreads and a nose ring. The crowd danced and swayed as the vibe went hip-hop gospel. Many closed their eyes and sang along, or threw their hands overhead, or let tears flow for Jesus. *Let the praises ring!* Sometimes Cherry deeply felt the worshipful ecstasy of the collective, letting the music carry her. Sometimes she even felt something akin to sex, a crescendo, the fervor of people starved for a large force to pervade them.

Sometimes she lost herself there. That was what drew her to Randy in the first place. Not God. Not Jesus. That dark and open...emptiness.

How could Randy enjoy what she did with his Golden Banana and still talk about temptation? Was he using her to get to God? Or to avoid Him? Did he think their sex was morally wrong? How could he not?

I mean, really. You're just turning him into the biggest sinner ever.

Suddenly she felt like a godless slut, like a Jezebel in her stupid yellow sweater. Her face grew hot and her confusion swept up, up into the crowd, floating away on a sea of *hallelujah.*

Chapter Three: *Jeremy*

I used to be someone.

I used to have someone.

I stare at my eyes in the mirror, unable to recognize myself. *Where have I gone?* Fuck if I know. Amy used to say my eyes looked like the jungle. A multitude of greens, a bit dangerous. Something lurking.

I'm on a hard surface. Dark. Could be night. Could be I've blacked out. Not sure. Feels like cement. My mouth tastes of the sour aftertaste of alcohol. Dry. I perceive a wavy blue line and a wavy red line and I realize that together they say COORS LIGHT. Ah: my friend Tommy's basement. I've been crashed here the past few weeks, praying every night not to wake up in the morning because I just don't know how to save myself. *I pray the Lord my soul to take.* But I just keep. On. Living.

It's a personal affront. I can't even fucking *die.*

Used to have a nice house. A decent job. Amy. I supervised the warehouse at an electronic parts manufacturer. Worked hard. My guys respected me. Worked at the plant for eight years, throwing boxes, and liking the work, never thinking twice. Until that goddamn bank crisis. We should have known, man. The free-wheeling, high-rolling days could only last so long. It was so big, like a herd of invisible buffalo we never saw coming. My neighbors and friends just woke up one day and *blam.* Lost jobs, retirement funds crashing, can't pay the mortgage, running up the credit cards, all while some suits on TV are telling us they don't know how this happened, how it was just a handful of bad, bad guys speculating with our hard-earned money like gamblers at the roulette wheel. How it *wasn't their fault.*

Sure as hell was somebody's fault.

How could money just disappear like that? From a bank, from the biggest of banks? They built a house of cards on me and on people like me, on our sore *backs,* and at least in my case, it fucked my life over. Once my job was gone, Amy and I faltered. Or I faltered as she watched: I'm not sure anymore. She began to mistrust me, to make me feel small inside. We were no longer equals. Seems that the only thing that ever made me her equal was the fact that I could hold my own.

Maybe she never really loved me.

"Jeremy. You home, bud?" Tommy's voice from the top of the stairs. I ignore it.

I remember being on my knees, trying to light the tricky gas fireplace in our bedroom. Amy came in, still in her work clothes, a dark blue dress with tan flowers. The fireplace started with a safety switch you had to press in and turn at the same time, like a medicine bottle. I tried the push and turn, push and turn until my knees ached and she urged me to the side with her knee. Her knee! In her fancy work dress she coaxed flames, letting out a frustrated breath with the first crackle. She was success-ful where I was not.

The violet violence itched through each layer of my skin. I wanted to lash out and yet, I wasn't that kind of man.

Not then.

Couldn't talk straight, my thoughts bleating out in ridiculous chopped sentences. "Amy, lately you're acting like. It's just that! Hey. Shit. You didn't give me a chance. You're being. I'm trying. I mean, I mean, you're acting like the fucking *dude* in this rela-tionship. Like nothing gets done unless you do it."

"Sometimes I wonder if I am the dude," she said, standing up and brushing her palms, holding my gaze for a split second before her eyes flashed away. I felt dismissed. She didn't have to say anything else. Lately I couldn't get it up anymore. *Is that what she meant?* Couldn't even give her the one thing I had left to offer her.

The shame was incredible.

From my primo spot on the basement floor, I make out the loud notes of Phil Collins' "In the Air Tonight" pouring down the stairs, over the old green and yellow braided rug, up and over a pool table, across the old tube TV, and into my aching head. Why couldn't Tommy play another song? Like I'd love to hear Stevie Ray Vaughn wailing. Some good blues. Instead, those eerie drums float on 80's synthesizer notes, drawn way out like taffy, evoking danger. It's like being lost in space, without gravity in an endless field of blue and black. *Wipe off that grin,* Phil says.

Under the music, the faint sound of Tommy and his girlfriend fucking: his grunts, her moans. My mind supplies an unwanted vision of her on her back, small breasts with upturned button nipples, Tommy holding her knees as he plows her, his ass thrusting. They don't even sound real. They don't even sound human.

God, it's like a kick in the stomach knowing what they're doing.

My cock throbs, angry and lonely.

The cold of the cement floor has seeped into my buttocks, through my jeans, and spread to my entire body. Outside the window, I spy the ostrich in a garish pool of light from the front porch. I've decided this specimen is a female because she looks so soft and graceful. Tonight she's just a blur of feather rushing by. Maybe if I caught her, I could mate with her. What would an ostrich feel like inside?

Maybe I'm becoming an ostrich and I don't know it.

I turn my head to the side and curl up in a ball, cupping my junk.

ॐॐ

So. Yeah. Anyway.

My days are spent in relative isolation, in hiding. I'd do anything – anything! – to have to have another job but I've sent out all these resumes and nothing's coming back and with every passing day, a little bit more of me leaks away like water into thirsty earth, leaving behind a scaly rime of anger. Nobody is buying stuff now, so there are no boxes of excess merchandise to store in my old warehouse, nothing to move with my forklift. I loved that forklift, the satisfying *whirr* of metal arranging pallets into ordered rows marked with bright yellow paint on the floor. The easy routine I'd established. Cup of coffee, one cream at 8:05am sharp with my guys in the break room.

I feel lost. I feel I don't belong. To any place. To anyone.

It is one of the worst sensations in the world: the windy carelessness of the lone wolf who badly wants a pack. I want my fucking pack.

It's too cold to be outside. If it were warm, I'd lay on the grass at the park. Instead, I hang at the library, escaping winter's bite with the homeless, jobless, and college students. Those who haven't started their lives and those who have dropped out. The students are the best. Tinny, happy notes of music trickle from their headphones as they sip hot drinks and munch pretzels. Sexting and starting online businesses between classes. So forward-moving, even while just sitting. So engrossed, not giving a shit about anything beyond the technology-soaked, infinitely-connected spheres where they exist. I like that. No ruse.

Hot college girls.

They contort into pink purple green yellow curled up shapes in chairs, tight jeans accentuating hips and sculpting crotches. I see myself kneel between a girl's legs right there in front of everyone, her cotton underwear at her ankles, parting her like perfect bluejean butterfly wings, the citrusy taste of her cunt on my tongue. Then I am distracted, my head whipping up comically to see delectable asses flowing by in lazy pairs. Assaulted on all sides by their tits and butts, I can barely withstand it. Snippets of songs flash as I turn the dial on the dirty radio station in my head. *Radar Love, Rock and Roll Hootchie Koo, Kick Start My Heart, Feel Like Makin' Love. Lube my cock, baby, wet it, stroke it, suck it, just watch me fill nasty little slut asses with my meat, taking them one after another bareback, whore moans escaping shiny tiny whore mouths when they feel my grown-up shaft shove into their most secret holes, bending those colorful bluejean girls over and over and over and over a table where six sternly identical studious brunettes type in unison on laptops, a row of brunettes stretching out into infinity, teeth bared in want, showing wet red lipstick, waiting to be fucked in the face or ass…*

My desire is boundless. I am ashamed and elated to have these thoughts. The last few months with Amy I couldn't perform. Now I seem to have a permanent boner and any contact with women ignites crazy fantasies. I think a lot about anal. Ass fucking. Amy didn't like it and we only did it twice. But I'd loved it. Teasing myself into that impossibly sweet little hole. It felt wild and uncharted, like I was taking her virginity. I'd never felt closer to her. I think about fucking one of the co-eds in the ass now, my cock buried to the hilt, my hands holding hips…

I stroll, book held artfully in front of my crotch, to the men's room. And only pump my cock a few times before I gush. I come out with a flushed face and clean hands, able to think again.

The magazine section is the best spot at the library.

The chairs are big and soft and I can skim through *Bon Appetit* and *Conde Nast Traveler* and imagine that my life is chock full of the wondrous places and delightful foods these publications describe. Chewy Chocolate Gingerbread. Salmon with a White Wine Reduction. Osso Bucco. What people are eating and doing in London, Tokyo, LA. What is "right now." *Do people really live like this? Get on a plane for eight hours to tour the lavender-scented countryside, trying fine wines and searching high and low for the best Coq au Vin in France? Are you shitting me? Someone does that?*

Huh. Our buildings, fabrications, asphalt, bits and bytes. The endless distractions of the fucking human race.

But we're just animals playing at life.

What distinguishes me from wolf, stray dog, ostrich? A thin membrane of culture, bullshit diversion that humans have gathered about ourselves to prove just how evolved we are: internet, television, art, books, iPhones, architecture, fast food, whipped cream, air travel, Facebook, washing machines. We are Michelangelo and we are McDonalds: how can this be so? How can we be both?

If it weren't for all that, we'd be eating and sleeping and fucking and hunting and howling just like the other beasts. Probably happier, too. Poetry never got me anywhere. I never ate any haute cuisine. I've never been to Paris. I have no need for Bed, Bath, and Beyond. I don't even have a bed of my own. I can barely clothe myself. All culture ever did for me was take my money and run.

Why can't I get a break? I want some measure of basic comfort. I want to stop running from place to place as friends get tired of having me on their couches and eventually kick me out. Nine beds in four months gets goddamn old. I want to know that when I spend some cash, I'll end up with more than $4.30 left in the bank. I want to take off the yoke of the credit card companies, drowning me in interest charges. I want to feel like a man again, to have something useful to do with my hands, the yawning empty space from sunup to sundown.

I'm not a bad guy. I do yearn for a woman, my own woman, a woman that I love who loves me back. Yearn to fall into her for hours, and I mean real love with birds and harps and valentines, to have her suck my cock until I come, to make her see stars, and then hold her nestled in a bed of dry, warm leaves in the forest, keeping her safe and making her mine.

Chapter Four: *Cherry*

Cherry lay on the bed with long arms angled overhead, a watercolor painting in swirls of curls and ivory flesh. Candles flickered on her nightstand and on the dresser. She was topless, with just a purple lace thong below, the smallest slip of fabric. Light from the windows was petal-pink from falling snow. It was perfect.

So where was Randy, already? She fidgeted, fingered herself.

She'd been ravenous all day, knowing she'd be penetrated that night, prowling like a tigress in heat at the bank. At lunch, she watched Eric, the sexy bank teller, eat a sandwich. She was fixated on his mouth, his generous lips. His hands were square and strong-looking, his ass tight in sensible khaki pants as he left the break room. On a conference call, her knees wiggled under the desk, phantom lips on her lips. *What was that, Tony? Yes, I have the quarterly report. I'll email it over now. Right after this kiss, this kiss...*

On the drive home she blasted the R & B station and sang along to thumping songs about knocking boots.

She rubbed her own nipple, flashing back to her younger self. Before she knew sex, only a hazy burn existed. A fire for no reason she could finger, an ache she wasn't sure how to fill, a question finally answered when she was 15 years old, kissing her boyfriend on his motorcycle in front of her house, in the rain, both of them soaked through to the bone but unable to stop reveling in the taste touch smell of one another. Things were so simple then! Sucking face and having *a boy like you*! Holding hands, passing notes, letting him grab your breasts or trace your pussy through your jeans if you *really* liked him. *Once blowjobs and fucking are a part of the scene,* Cherry mused, *good old heavy petting doesn't seem to contain the same magic.*

Her burn was all grown up now, no longer innocent haze but full-on interstellar starburst, impossible to ignore.

She heard Randy's footsteps on the stairs, the door softly opening as if through clouds, as if edged open by an angel's wing. *Finally!* Cherry was ready to kick things up a notch. She had silk scarves in the drawer. Maybe she'd even get Randy to let her suck him. She wanted to learn. She wanted to fly.

"Baby," he said, crossing the room with the same lissome, professional movement he showed onstage, a vapor trail of tiny sparkles following his form. Cherry wondered if she should have had that second strong drink as the stars swirled. He jumped on the bed, his tongue sliding straight into her vodka mouth. The stars floated and dispersed like confetti. She kissed greedily, coarse noises escaping her. He traced her as slow as molasses, caressing nipples, hips, and insides of thighs.

"Get on top of me," Cherry said, tugging his boxers down over his erection. "I've been wet for a half hour." *Who is this animal inside me? I love her.*

"Slow," he answered, circling a finger around her belly button, tracing her like a 15-year-old would, connecting the dots on her breasts. He brushed her hand away like *baby, I'm running this show here* but he wasn't. He was too caring, too focused on being tender. Cherry just wanted to be fucked. Hard. Pinned to the bed by the weight of her man, impaled by him. Her pussy raged and ached to be filled, *filled* with more than smooth jazz and a smooth touch, to be poured to the brim with force and life and everything that is hard, fast, and solid.

Solid: so she would know for certain she existed.

❧

But there was someone else.

Where Randy was polished and composed, Red was earthy, sexy, sloppy, and loudly funny, a man from a big Italian family who was used to having to make a splash to be heard.

When Cherry first met him, he brought flowers. She called him Red for his dark red hair and beard – and eyes the impossible color of a chestnut stallion. He stood in front of the museum, a building of steel and glass, wrapped in a jaunty striped scarf like a European, clutching a bouquet of Stargazer lilies and peering at her with eyes that sent intelligent, lusty sparks. His masculinity took her by surprise and she found herself loving him with wild immediacy but not trusting the feeling. *Because only a player brings flowers on a first date.*

They spent hours together browsing the exhibits, eating lunch, talking about everything and nothing, and when they ran out of things to do at the museum, they went to a café, their conversation an excuse to look at and circle each other. In front of a fireplace with glowing logs and paintings of moose, they held hands and he told her that he wanted to make her happy and bring her pleasure.

She was speechless.

The next day, one of the lilies bloomed in an unmistakable display of sexual fervor, mirroring what Cherry felt inside for Red. She had been unable to sleep since they'd started emailing. He made her vagina – her, her *pussy* – feel awake and demanding. The lily was white, as big as her head, and the sweet-smelling petals were scalloped like the ruffles of a dancer's fancy dress. Its stamens were coated with brick-colored pollen that looked like dried blood on her hands.

His goodbye kiss had been more passionate and satisfying than all the sex she'd ever had with her other lovers, whose numbers were few. Through his coat and hers, she'd felt his hard cock pushing outward. Red's mouth took her, told her he desired her, in no uncertain terms, and left her wanting only to be completely possessed by him.

If it hadn't been so bitterly cold and isolated in the dark parking lot, they would have made love right there in the back seat of the car, breath fogging the windows and cries piercing the silence with the animal joy of two lost mates finding each other.

She just knew it.

৵ৎ৵

Lunch break.

Cherry sat in her car at the grocery store, eye makeup running down her cheeks and dripping onto her nice work shirt. She didn't wipe it, didn't blow her nose, didn't move to become more composed or presentable in any way, her breath shuddering out between sobs and her face wet with sadness. She observed the people with their carts, hefting sacks of food into their yawning trunks. Mothers positioning baby seats. Men carrying twelve-packs of beer. People talking on cell phones. *Why am I not content the way I was before?* Cherry thinks.

Then she thinks: *because I want a man like Red. A real man, with big shoulders that look like they could tackle a buffalo, a man who can lift me. A cocky man who owns his woman and his sexuality. A man who will let me lose all control.*

Randy orchestrated his life, down to the loving. They never totally let go together. And she didn't trust his, trust his lightweight ass with the way she needed to be…fucked. That was the word. *Fucked.* She smiled at herself. Not sex and certainly not making love.

I should try using this word more. Fuck, fucked, fucking.

It wasn't just the sex. It was that she was just sailing along with Randy, unmoored, lost and watching herself like a bad movie.

After the goodbye kiss with Red, they'd smiled at each other, the spicy prospect of sex in the air like a fine lilac mist. If she let him, he could rock her world! She leaned in, ready for more, but his face began to pixelate ever so slowly, losing definition. Soon she only saw the creamy brown of his eyes streaming away like warm chocolate through the air. Cherry cried out, feeling herself soar upwards as if pulled by a puppet's strings. She struggled against this force, trying to hold on to the man and the moment, the possibility of their love as sweet as a just-cut fruit. But Red faded, disappeared. A piercing yellow light filled every corner of her field of vision.

And she woke up with a mournful start, alone in her bedroom on a sunny morning, realizing Red was a dream.

Remembering this, Cherry closed her eyes and laid her head on the steering wheel. Losing it.

She screamed. Screamed again.

And dialed Becca on her cell.

ॐ᪵

"Late, late, sorry, sorry!" Becca sang, settling onto a barstool at The Tornado in a flurry of scarf and jacket. Her dress was red with white flowers and a wide leather belt at the hips, and her hair was up in pigtails. The dress hid nothing and highlighted everything. Compared to Cherry in her crisp blue suit, Becca looked radiant and uninhibited, ten pounds over what the magazines might call ideal: a delicious and perfect erotic nymph. *Men are programmed to like curves,* Becca liked to say. *I'm going to eat my butter, my chocolate, my steak and fuck what Cosmo has to say about it.* A nymph who didn't compromise. She smiled and grabbed a bite of eggroll from a plate on the bar, crunching it in her mouth with obvious pleasure.

"I already ordered us glasses of chardonnay," Cherry said, dipping a dumpling into sauce with her chopsticks. "And eggrolls, two kinds of dumplings, and beef sticks."

The bartender, a slim gay man named Steve, looking even slimmer in black slacks and a black shirt, came over to greet them with double-cheek kisses as he always did.

The sun was sinking as the happy-hour crowd started to arrive. Cherry used the word *breakdown* on the phone with Becca. So Becca called for an emergency pow-wow – complete with food and adult beverages.

"I'm usually the one with the troubles," Becca said. "Talk to me, sweetie."

Cherry motioned at Steve with her glass and he gave her another pour of wine. "The last time we went out, you never answered my question. About Terence."

"You mean when you were loading me into a cab? All sloshed and sorry over that dickweed? You'll have to remind me."

"How was he? Um, in bed?" Cherry asked.

"This is the emergency reason you had to see me?"

"Becca!"

"Huh. Ok. Gorgeous. That's why I put up with his shit, I guess. Really adventurous. Funny and fun." Becca paused. "Sure you want to get into details? You know I'm down with the sexy talk but *you've* never been the type to want to chat about the horizontal rumba."

"Go on." *I am the type now. Horizontal rumba, sex, fucking, intercourse: whatever you want to call it. I am the type, damn it.*

A slow and sultry grin oozed over her friend's face, painting a glowing picture of the nights of sweaty passion with Terence. Much more so than words could express. Cherry cringed a little. Inside. "He loved for me to dress up for him. You know. Um, little schoolgirl, nurse, sexy librarian. Nothing but a white shirt and man's tie. Nothing but a pair of tall boots. Stuff like that. Big heels. Big hair. Even leather. He took his time. He'd eat my pussy for hours if I wanted. And he loved toys."

"Toys. *Gulp.* You used toys?"

"Oh, yeah. He liked me to do him with a strap-on sometimes. And I have a whole box full of dildos. Cock rings. Flavored oils…"

"Strap…on," Cherry said deliberately, assaulted by new knowledge about what a man and woman might do together. She felt like she'd been sucker-punched. She'd never used any toy with herself, let alone Randy. Her sex life with him was flat. Light foreplay, penis, vagina. Terence and Becca dressed up, played with toys, laughed.

She never laughed anymore, in bed or out.

Red had told her jokes. Dream jokes to make her dream giggle.

"Cherry? Don't you use toys with Randy? Or try anything new? Things always seemed great between you. I mean, he's so sweet, capable, good-looking. He's so put-together. So *you*."

Cherry moaned like a hurt animal.

"Shit, I knew this was too much for you to handle," Becca said.

"No. No! I *want* to talk about sex. *I want to.* If I can actually talk about it, I may be able to feel something more. Sexually. You know? Even feel something more in my whole *life*. There's something inside me waiting to be found. I want to laugh in bed. Scream! With pleasure! I bet you scream with pleasure every time, don't you? A lot of times – hell, most times – I hold my breath and get so anxious I can't even come!" Once Cherry started sharing she couldn't stop, even though her voice was breaking, even though her heart was knocking a terrible rhythm in her chest. "Hearing about the toys is fucking awful and horrid because I know I've been settling for this dead, dry relationship. We hardly make love anymore. We did it last weekend but before that, it had been *six weeks*. My whole body is so tense and dried out that even when I try to make love, it takes like 45 minutes for me to really open up. And he never wants to do anything good, anyway. We don't have any toys. You know, I've never given him a blow job, *anyone* a blow job. I was scared of it, you know, gagging or something, but I wanted to try and Randy said no! He acted like I was a whore, almost, just for asking. Then he turns around and tells me our lack of sex might be my brain chemistry, that I should get on antidepressants or go to his Christian therapist friend. Am I a whore or am I frigid? He said he's not the one with the issue *but I know he feels guilty because we aren't married* and God says it's a sin. He's sinning with me. The thing is: he doesn't do it for me and I don't think he ever did, no matter how much I deny it!" She drank in breath.

Becca reached right over and wrapped Cherry in her tattooed arms, hugging hard. "Sweetie, why didn't you tell me this before?"

"Because I thought something was wrong with me."

"Nothing is wrong with you. You guys aren't compatible. As simple as that. You have every right to figure out what makes you happy. And if it's not him, it's better for both of you if you leave."

"I want to feel something more. I want more. I want…." Her voice trailed off as she ran out of juice, slumping on the barstool.

Becca hugged her again. "Let Becca help you." To the bartender: "Two tequila shots right here, Steve."

❧❦

Sufficiently liquored up, they went to an adult store for inspiration. Becca's idea.

Cherry was rubbing a plastic dress between her fingers with childlike wonder. The material squeaked loudly. It was fire red, with short sleeves and metal snaps all the way down, so it could be ripped open.

Becca nodded sagely, with approval, as if Cherry were seriously considering it. "Those rock. I had a guy actually get on his knees and kiss my feet when I wore one to a club. Like I was some kind of damn goddess in PVC. The power of the plastic dress cannot be underestimated, Cher. Men die for it. Something about your body encased in plastic and easy access. The big reveal. Like they can just tear it open and savage you in an alley." She surveyed the other clothing. "Or how about this crotchless number? Oooh, or look: sexy leather goth bikini!" This was little more than ribbon and tiny black triangles printed with spiderwebs. Becca held it up and danced it in front of Cherry.

Cherry shook her head, moving on wordlessly, reverently, moving as if magnetized to a huge wall of vibrators lit with bluish track lighting. Every shape and size, color and texture imaginable. Some looked like penises and some were animals: dolphin, teddy bear, tiger, rabbit. Cherry shuddered at the thought of sticking a dolphin in her pussy and picked up the tiger, which had a tail sticking out and gold beads inside some squishy gel. *Cutting Edge Orgasm Technology,* the package promised. *Orgasm technology?* thought Cherry.

The clerk, a stunning black woman in an electric-blue leather bustier and matching thigh-high boots, came to help. "Customer favorite," she said, taking the tiger and turning it on. The whole thing vibrated and the tail gyrated and the beads wiggled inside the gel. "Looks crazy as hell but damn does this thing fly off the shelf. Women can't get enough of this shit." Her big gold hoop earrings glinted under the track lighting.

Becca said, "I think something more like, ah, the real thing."

Blue Bustier pointed to a massive, flesh-colored cock. "How about this one? We call it Kong. For ladies who like them some extra."

"Too big...," Cherry said. *Could all of that really go inside me?* Blue kept showing Cherry the top sellers.

"...too hard."

"...too *veiny*."

"...too...ewwww!"

Becca burst out laughing. "You're a dirty Goldilocks!"

Cherry smiled, waving a vibrator. "This one's *just right*." It was bright red, shaped like a cock but much thicker than anything she'd personally experienced. Bright red. *Red.* She kept running her hand over it and switching between speed settings.

Becca said, "We'll take that one! Oh, and one of those little pink g-spot things. She needs one of those."

"Gimme the tiger, too," Cherry added, giggling.

When they left, unmarked pink paper bags in hand, Cherry felt like she was going on an adventure.

๛

Cherry is lying square in the middle of her queen bed, on top of the green blanket printed with leaves. She's naked and dissolving with laughter. Completely and thoroughly and deliciously taken, surfing the aftershock of a frenzied fantasy, a good and nasty ride. Every bit of her body was alive. And singing.

When she got home with her goodies, Cherry peeled them open, spending some time curiously marveling over their forms. She inserted batteries and laid them on the bed, like a chef might lay out his knives and spoons. Then she took a hot bath. As she lay in the tub, she turned her head to the side and saw the neat row of vibrators waiting for her. She smiled.

She didn't bother to put clothes on.

She chose the thick red cock, circling it with her hand, and lowered herself onto the mattress and into juicy, uncharted territory. She turned the vibrator on and touched the head to her clit. The sensation was so strong she could feel it in her toes and in her teeth, so she turned it down one notch. Better. Began swiveling the cock against herself in slow circles.

In her mind's eye, Randy entered the darkened room unbidden and found her naked on the bed, curled up with her new treasure. *What are you doing?* he sputtered. *What the hell is that?* She shooed him off impatiently, his voice trailing, and let another image spill onto the screen as softly as a puff of solitary cloud on the breeze. A small cabin in the woods at night, pristine snowdrifts and tall pines. She stood silhouetted in the window in a long robe of black silk, peering out into the winter night.

MMM. She slid the cock in and made love to herself for a while, spiraling and sliding the vibrator until her pussy felt swollen. *Jesus, I thank you for the blessing of this toy…*

Her heart thumped like a monkey in a cage. She took the cock out, put it against her lips, hesitated, felt herself tensing. She closed her eyes and took a deep breath, two deep breaths, calming. *My virgin mouth.* Inserted the fat tip inside her mouth gradually, feeling incredibly dirty. She gasped and took it back out. Just putting the tip in had caused a wild reaction, her chest arching up towards the ceiling, her pussy calling loudly for *more.* She opened her mouth hungrily, sliding the shaft further, opening to the girth of it, further, grasping it by the base, further, delirious with the new sensation of cock in her throat. It took a few minutes to relax her throat fully and breathe yet her body knew what to do, instinctively. It was easy, natural, exciting.

Oh, *fuck this is good.*

Whenever she approached her edge, she pulled the cock out. She sensed the adventure was meant to be savored, not rushed.

The Cherry inside the cabin moved away from the window, smoothness of silk in her walk and against her skin. She thought she'd heard something outside but it must have been the wind. She poured a glass of Pinot Gris and sat on the floor in front of the fireplace for a while, the warmth of the flames on her skin. Then, a knock on the door.

Oh, my. Who could that be at this time of night, all the way out here? She cracked the door, leaving the chain on. Two men in snowsuits stood on the porch, their faces red, ice in their eyelashes. The one with blue eyes said, "Miss? Any way we could warm up? Our snowplow broke down and we're plumb stuck."

Cherry put coffee on and the men peeled off their wet outer layers in her mudroom, coming out in t-shirts and jeans. They were young and muscled. Blue Eyes – Joe – had blonde hair and was a little shorter and boxier, like a wrestler. The other one, Sam, was lean and wiry, with hazel eyes and brown hair. In front of the fire they sipped coffee, the men thawing out on either side of her on the couch. They made small talk about the weather and then fell silent, watching the fire. After a while, Joe smiled and fished something out of his jeans pocket.

Being stuck in a cabin with stranded snowplow drivers was her most favorite fantasy and with the vibrator it was so, so much better...

The walls of her pussy pulsed against the silicone cock and she licked her hand, putting wet fingers to her nipple.

"Cherry, do you mind?" Joe said, revealing a small glass pot pipe. *Pot – another thing she'd never done that she wanted to try. Why not? Why not do it ALL?*

Warm, cozy, two beautiful young men. "Only if I can have the first hit," she said, smiling. Joe leaned over to her, holding the pipe to her mouth with his hand. She held his wrist suggestively, sucked in, held the smoke. The men both smiled. "Shit yeah," said Sam, taking a long hit and then laughing.

Men of few words.

The pot worked its way from Cherry's mouth to her edges in about eight seconds. She became acutely aware that she was naked under the robe and that her nipples were hard and her pussy was tingling and that the men knew it like the lions know the lioness is in heat. "Music?" Joe asked, going over to her stereo, flipping through her CDs. He inserted one and Bob Marley's "Could You Be Loved" came on. The blonde man shook his ass, strutted across the living room, dancing in reggae time while Sam and Cherry nodded along. Cherry bounced up, stopping to take a hit off the pipe that Joe held out. Sam grasped her waist and pulled her close, moving with her as Joe watched, his dark eyes turning hot. The smoke had removed all her inhibitions and Cherry slapped Sam on the ass, springing away as he grabbed at her. He was fast though, and he wrapped his arms around her and kissed her sweetly, meaningfully even, running his hand over her butt, kissed her until she had to break for air. Sam was not the one on her mind, however.

She slithered over to Joe, wiggling in front of him, licking her lips like a porn star. He watched calmly. She shimmied again, looking for his reaction. He waited ten beats, watching her watch him. He put his hands on her hips and reeled her into his lap. She could feel his dick through his jeans and she hummed as he kissed her neck and slowly bit her nipples through the silk, all while directing her hips back and forth over his hardness with the touch of one hand. He slowed, moaning a little, and she heard her breath drawing out, she *saw* her breath oozing from her mouth as hearts and moons and suns and stars and smiley faces. Sam was on the couch next to them, suddenly, his fly open, working his stick languidly with his eyes on Cherry. It was fat, with a purple head, and she wanted it, to feel it, touch it, taste it. Her robe was moist and she wondered if they could tell how wet she was.

climbing climbing climbing climbing

Joe surprised her, shoving a finger inside her enflamed pussy, picking up pace. She jolted and let her hips rock back and forth on him, her body no longer in her control. "Suck this thing," he said hoarsely, unbuttoning his jeans to reveal a huge, ropy cock. Cherry got to her knees and took him all the way to the hilt, grabbed his balls, ran the flat of her tongue up the length and then devoured him again. He sighed and she looked up at him. "Don't stop," he rasped.

Every time his dick filled her throat, growing larger and larger, her entire body pulsated and bucked. She couldn't believe how *pleasurable* it felt being penetrated this way, how powerful and feminine she felt with him in her mouth. The harder his erection became, the more she bloomed and surged around him like water, yielding where he was firm. From behind, she felt Sam's fingers part her and the velvety head of his cock nudging up against her lips. *Oh god oh yes oh please do it to me.* He pulled her hair and said *fucking your cunt baby,* his dick sliding in, caressing her completely from the inside. Cherry whimpered. They worked her over, worked her soulfully, worked her good, both of the beautiful men, sweating and grunting, she saw Joe smile at Sam as if he couldn't believe what was happening, Sam was slapping her thigh *kinda* hard and then *definitely* hard saying *riding this ass baby,* and pulling the shit out of her hair, and Joe's cock was slamming into her hungry hungry oh god hungry mouth and by necessity she left her body, becoming pure sheer sensation, pure cunt, pure want, all three of them shuddering and melting and trembling into each other, Joe moaning Cherry whimpering as he unloaded into her mouth with a hot salty gush, Sam's cock spurting over her ass.

OH.

OH GOD.

Cherry yelled hoarsely and a well of laughter, trapped inside since perhaps she was a little girl, exploded outwards. Laughed.

She laughed so long her ribs hurt.

She laughed so long her face hurt.

The forgotten vibrator lay on the bed to the side, buzzing.

Every bit of her body sang with a fulfillment she didn't know was possible, the men in the cabin fading, their jobs done, leaving nothing but Cherry – nude, peeled, flayed – tears leaking from her eyes.

That night, Red came back to her in her dreams.

Chapter Five: *Jeremy*

The boy went ahead, almost disappearing, his camouflage jacket and hat of brown and beige matching the dead winter foliage. The tops of the pine trees were the only spot of color, with their waving green tufts of needles. I pulled my boots through the mud with satisfaction, each step clinging wetly to the earth. Felt good. Some snow had melted on a surprise warm weekend, so I took my nephew for a hike in the woods.

The peace descended on me, tickling my nose with the scent of earth. Surrounded by the tall trunks, slogging through the wet, I forgot for a while. Forgot the running and moving and the sickly feeling I had every morning when I awoke without Amy and without the person I used to be. Without the things that used to define me, I was wide open for attack and felt like the whole world was hunting me down. And some really were hunting me down. Bill collectors, acting like if they only called me enough times, harassed me enough, I'd magically cough up the tens of thousands of dollars I owed them. The ghosts – real and imagined – of the shitty economy.

Tommy had asked me to leave. His girlfriend never had liked me and I suspected she was the reason he booted me from the basement, although he said he couldn't handle the extra utilities cost. She thought I was a sorry loser who wasn't even trying to find a job. Shit. No love lost there. I thought she was an ugly-hearted, aging hipster in fancy clothes who acted like she was doing Tommy a favor by being with him. Her tits were too small. And she was rude. And on the way out, I told him so. He cussed me but I was glad I said it. He needed the truth.

My brother George's place was better anyway. Instead of a ratty couch in a cold basement I had an actual bed, an old twin bed with a red paisley blanket and boy's sheets printed with space rockets. There was even space next to the bed for my suitcases and my box of CDs. A door I could close for privacy. As close to heaven as I could imagine, having been through what I had. And my brother was divorced, so there were no women around to disapprove of me, just me, George, and his 15-year-old, Caleb. All the beer I could drink and someone to play video games with all night if I wanted.

"Uncle J!" Caleb yelled. He'd stopped and was poking at something with a branch, stabbing dramatically as if the branch were a sword. I got closer and saw a snake coiled inside the mouth of a dead log, half-hidden under dry underbrush. "I think it's making a rattling noise!" he said, excited, taking a step back.

I looked at it. Gray, with a mottled black pattern and small scales that gave it a satin gleam. The snake moved, making a soft *crunch* in the leaves. "No, it's not a rattler. They have diamond-shaped heads and are more beige. Remember that. Diamond-shaped head. This guy is a black racer." Caleb, chest forward, was trying his best to stare the serpent down. Now that we'd established it wasn't deadly, he was brimming with teenaged bravado.

"I'm not a punk," he said. "That snake is a cunt."

"Don't use that word," I told him. "It's offensive."

He squared his shoulders at me. "What word? Punk, snake, or cunt?" Testing me.

"You *know* what word," I said tersely.

"My friend Joel called my girlfriend a cunt when she broke up with me."

"Like I said, it's rude and totally demeaning to women. Don't use it." I paused. "You'll never get a date that way, man. I mean, just find another word, OK? Like asshole or fuckwad or something."

"My dad said you called Amy a cunt when she left. He specifically mentioned the word "cunt." Can we use it when women hurt us? Is it ok then?"

What was his problem? The peace of the forest drained away and I felt the anger waking, rising, scalding my pelvis and breastbone. My mouth watered with invective, just aching to unload on the kid, to really let him have it. My lips opened.

Against my cheek, a gossamer wing brushed, making my breath catch. The ostrich! She stopped two feet in front of me. My throat closed.

She cocked her head and made a *tsk tsk* gesture with her wing. *Don't be mad at him. He's just repeating stuff he's heard. He's just asking about heartbreak. He's just flexing his muscles.* I heard her. I did! In my head I did, I heard her.

Caleb was busy, thwacking a tree with a large branch, brows knit. The ostrich and I had a mental conversation.

Jeremy. When are you going to get it?

Get what?

You are so much more than you think. You're strong, capable. An amazing man.

No. I am a zero. I am a zero balance. I have none of the stuff, none of that special green paper we honor so fucking much! I have no job. I have no woman. I have no home. I am a zero balance, total fucking loser.

Are you really measuring yourself by a pile of paper?

Well, shit. Yeah. Look at what Amy thought. Look at the world we live in. The size of your pile matters.

Forget what Amy thought. Forget the world. This is about the intensity of your heart. Her wing caressed my cheek. *Poor man!* I shrunk away from her.

I grabbed Caleb's shoulders and turned him roughly. "Do you see it?"

"See what?" he said, shaken by my grasp.

"You don't see it? It's right there, right there, mocking me, following me God DAMN it to all hell," I yelled, wrapping my arms in front of my chest, suddenly very cold. "It's right fucking THERE."

"Come on," he said. Then he pulled my coat, leading me away. "Let's go eat, chill out," my nephew said, concern in his eyes. I turned to look over my shoulder and saw only the flash of a gray tail.

My brother George's face loomed above mine and above him, afternoon shards of sun on the ceiling. "Awake?" he asked, lowering himself to a squat footstool next to the couch where I lay. Caleb was gone, leaving a scattered stack of pizza crusts and soda cans on the counter in his wake. I turned to my side to face George. Face the music. Whatever harsh, heavy words he'd unload like so many bricks.

But he was compassionate.

"Man, I know it's been hard on you," he started. "When the divorce went through with Betsy, her absence ate at me. Knocked me in the gut and ran me over every day. For months. I mean, I felt like I was seeing things sometimes. Not um, an ostrich. But I was fucked up. And you've got the whole job thing,"

I interrupted. "I have been looking. I have," I said.

"I know. Gotta start fresh, Jeremy. Try something different, something you haven't done before. Your old job is gone. The credit cards – well, I don't know. Let's look into bankruptcy, maybe. Look. We need a floor manager and I'll just pull some strings, get you in if I can. You can't just lay in the bed thirteen hours a day, or come home baked or leave home baked, or have shit around like this for Caleb to find." He held a crumpled piece of paper out to me. I unfolded it, read, smiled.

She slowly sucks my slick stick shudders and screams

When i cram her creamy candy dandy cunt full

"I thought it was some bitchin' alliteration, man," I said. "I mean, this is not a porno. What's the deal?"

"Dude. Get your head out of the fucking toilet. You need to get laid instead of, I don't know, writing pornographic poetry or whatever this shit is." He snort-laughed, despite himself. "Alliteration." He pulled on his beard, the way he did when he was trying to find an answer. "Maybe I can set you up with Beth."

"That brunette from the bowling alley?"

He slugged my shoulder and grinned in that way that said things were ok between us. Buddies. I was glad. "You don't wanna marry her. You just wanna fuck her."

Chapter Six: *Cherry*

"I can't," Cherry said.

"Can't what?" asked Randy.

"Can't do it anymore. Me. You. Us." She pressed her hands on the counter and switched the phone to the other ear. This was much harder than she expected. Her stomach hurt. She went to the refrigerator and grabbed a cold bottle of soda to soothe it.

Randy's voice was taut. "Cherry. Baby. You're just stressed out right now…"

"Now you say that. I've been stressed for months and you've barely noticed."

"I'm coming over," Randy said.

"No. Listen – you left some stuff at my place. I'm going to drop it off at your office at church. No one will know. No one will know how *involved* we were." Her voice cracked a little. He made a noise to interrupt her but she continued, her words tripping over themselves. "I mean, really, Randy. You have to be filled with contempt for me. I'm a sinner. With me, you were one, too." Cherry wiped her eye.

"I'm meant to be with you. God works in mysterious ways, Cherry."

"*Spare me the bullshit.* Are you really bringing that mysterious ways stuff out? You're an amazing guy but I just need more than you are able to give. Like, in every way. Don't you know how cold you are?

How keeping the lie going hurts me? How you make me feel like shit because you won't make love to me?"

"I'm – coming – over," he repeated, now with a note of urgency in his voice, and hung up.

Shit!

Cherry contemplated running away: to Becca's, to the store. Escape the awkward discussion. She curled up on the white couch to brood about it for a moment, twisting a lock of hair to help her think, but then he was already knocking on the door.

Cherry opened the door and Randy barged in, grabbing her in the type of hug he never usually gave: big and warm and meaningful. She stiffened though, disgusted. *Letting go is the right thing to do,* she thought. *Too little, too late.*

"Cherry, have you thought any more about the counseling? Richard says he can start seeing us," he started. Concerned. Caring. The preacher was on, helping guide her to the light.

"I don't want counseling. I don't need counseling. What's not working is *this relationship*, this secretive shit I've been settling for. I'm fucking done," she spat.

"Cherry!"

"I know, I know. Where's the good girl you first fell in love with in Bible study? Well, she doesn't exist, Randy. She was a ghost. I am a complicated woman. Not just a little girl. And I need more. Someone who can give me…give me." She worked to get the words out. "Give me the uninhibited, ah, *fucking* I need and can handle all the emotions I can dish out and can, I don't know, break me out of my shell and dance with me through life. You know?" She smiled now, at his shock and the hint of red anger rising into his face.

"I don't know what to say. You're not making sense. I can get you some help," Randy said, struggling. "I haven't been making love to you because, well, I feel like we should wait. Should have waited. I feel very wrong about it. I know we were doing it – but I think we should have waited. Until marriage."

Cherry said, "You know, I don't even think I like Jesus anymore."

Randy put his hand on hers and she shook it off. He said, "We all have days where we feel far from Him." He was much more comfortable with her not liking Jesus than her saying the f-word.

"No. This isn't about feeling far from Him. This 's about wondering if I ever believed in Him. Where has Jesus been while we've been having premarital sleepovers? Where was Jesus when I had to lay off half of my department? Since the downturn, we can barely make our numbers. And there were *protesters* in front of the bank this week. All week. Can you believe it? This Occupy thing. And they were pissed off. I've been praying about it, hard. The whole thing is crazy and I know it's not related to us but maybe it is because breaking up with you – it's kind of like I'm breaking up with Jesus, too. Maybe I'm breaking up with the whole fucking lot."

From the kitchen table, Cherry grabbed a brown paper bag which held Randy's random flotsam: a few shirts, some CDs, a toothbrush. She thrust it at him and folded her hands across her chest.

"Randy. I'm sorry. Please."

When he didn't move, she took his arm and steered him out the door. "Please," she repeated. He turned to her, now pale, the bag clutched against his chest.

"Stay with me. Marry me," he said.

Cherry was shocked, and could only shut the door on his frozen look.

❧

Becca's apartment pulsed with the happy beats of African pop. Her head was in the fridge and her rear end in a zebra-print skirt stuck out. "What's your poison? Coke, Corona, pineapple juice? Or do you need a really good stiff one?"

Cherry lay on the floor in a big old t-shirt of Becca's, sinking into a soft rag rug, looking up at the Christmas lights strung around the living room. They'd just gone over what had happened, down to Randy's desperate parting marriage proposal. And Cherry's breakup with Jesus.

"Stiff one. Ha ha," she said lazily.

"Ha ha," Becca echoed.

Cherry said, "Coke."

Becca came out with a huge glass of soda with lots of ice and a colorful bendy straw. Cherry sat up and sipped gratefully as Becca smoothed her hair. Her stomach ached with confusion.

"It's like I'm a sick little girl and you're taking care of me," Cherry said.

Becca pat her hand. "You are and I am."

"It's just – how can this feel so bad when I wanted to let go of him? All I wanted was to be free of him and I feel shitty."

"Maybe it's just that frustrating fear of being alone," Becca said.

They were both silent. The music played.

"Um, do you have some pot on you?" Cherry said, not looking at Becca. Becca crawled over, though, and peered right into her face with an evil grin. "You've never asked before. I mean, I've got some good shit. But Cher, are you sure?"

"Yes. I'm desperate to forget myself for a while. Forget Randy. Forget the crap at work and the pressure of everyone hating me because I work at a bank. I'm frantic. I need it." She nodded to her friend: *It's ok. I understand what I'm doing here. I'm going over my edge.*

She shut her eyes for a few minutes. The music changed to something bluesy and low-key. Becca was back, now in PJs, too: green and white polka dots like a little girl might wear. She handed Cherry a big orange water pipe.

"OK, sister, I'm gonna hook you up. So, you put your mouth right here. When I light it, inhale deep and hold it in for a moment."

Cherry allowed a little smile. She followed Becca's instructions. The hot smoke burned and she started coughing right away. Torture! "Again," Becca said. "Just more slowly." Cherry held the smoke in and let it out and as she did, all the tension she'd felt with Randy, all the tension she'd maybe *ever* felt in her life, just melted away. Her eyes fell on a black and white photo poster of a nude woman Becca had on a wall, a present from a former love.

"That woman's *ass* is just to die for," she said, pointing, rolling back into the delicious nest of pillows they'd created on the rug.

Becca let her breath go, exhaling into laughter. "You're so stoned, Cherry Jones."

"Fuck yeah, I'm stoned. And it feels…" Cherry searched for a word but then her mind zoned on the song that was playing and how amazing the bass line was and how the guitar was in perfect harmony.

Becca laughed at her.

Cherry said, "I love how I feel right now. I love it. My body is like *TA DA!* and I can even feel this goodness in my *toes,* you know what I'm saying?" She wiggled her toes at Becca to show her. Everything was better high. The music. The colors. She giggled. *This pot stuff is as good as I always imagined it. I am going to start smoking this like, regular.*

"Uh huh," murmured Becca. "Toes. That's good. You dizzy or anything?"

"No. Yes. Maybe a little. Gimme my soda." Everything was moving really, really slow. She grabbed Becca's hand. "I was so scared to break it off with Randy because I don't want to be alone. That's the dirty secret. I am petrified to be alone. And this is the BEST soda I have ever had. Like, ever. It's so sweet and fizzy and perfect and why don't I drink MORE of this? Know what I really need?"

Becca lay down next to her, her dreadlocked head against Cherry's. "What? Cookies?"

"No. To be HELD."

Becca scooted close and wrapped her friend so they were spooning.

"Thanks, Bec. Yeah, like that." She snuggled in closer, marveling at how wonderful it felt. How warm their bodies were together. "But I mean just HELD in every sense of the word. Held. I want to be held! I need to be held! I feel like I'm out there alone in the world, like even when I'm with coworkers or whatever, it's just ME. My family is so far away and it's not like we're close. There's just YOU and ME, Becca. And mostly ME. I'm not afraid to admit it, damn it! I AM MOTHERFUCKING LONELY!"

Becca rubbed Cherry's tummy. "You're never alone, Cherry. You are connected to everyone on the planet. In the universe. We're all one."

Cherry pondered this through the ganja haze. *Connected to everyone? Like one big cosmic string of pearls?* She grinned up at the ceiling while her friend rose to get them snacks.

Red, if you're out there, I'm here. I'm waiting for you. I'm the 459th pearl. I invite you to come and get me.

"Becca!" she yelled. "Come back in here and hold me some more!"

Chapter Seven: *Jeremy*

How do I get out of this?

So I'm in a white button-up shirt and nice slacks, crouched behind a trash can in my ex-wife's backyard, peeping her having dinner with some fucking guy. Some guy, oh shit, *some guy*. She's just opened the back door to let in fresh air and the round scent of roast meat wafts out. She's holding a glass of red wine and wearing a yellow dress that loves her hips, just loves 'em. The sight of her body shimmering in that color, the ease of her, the glorious curves. I sense my body (not just the obvious part) rising up, wanting to meet her.

Hollywood Woman on her toes, I bet.

I'm so hungry. For the roast, for a leading role in the romantic dinner scene, for a home of my own where I can relax. For Amy.

How do I get out of this?

I started a job where my brother works – a home improvement store. I thought I'd be roaming the aisles, taking boxes down for folks, demonstrating equipment, driving a forklift. Things I know. I know everything about tools and do-it-yourself. Turns out I'm mostly sitting in a windowless office in the back, wearing a monkey suit and doing emails and inventory reports. I hate it. Hate. It. I know it's a job and all and my brother is so proud and it gives me something to do but I fucking want to bash someone's skull in. It's not the right job. The right job, I'd be using my hands. I'd be a man, not a machine.

How do I get out of this?

OK. Right. Breathe. I have 20 minutes to get to my date with Beth. Bowling Alley Beth. Maybe she'll like the business shirt and gray slacks.

I glance back in at Amy and the guy, a tall blonde with blue eyes. He looks a little light and fruity to me. Bet he sits in an office all day too. But the *way she touches him*: fingertips brushing his arm when she laughs, wiping something off his cheek, a caress of the shoulder. Oh shit I feel like nothing nobody kaput fucked trapped alone. It's over. Really. She's moved on. She's forgotten. She's wiped her hands of someone who couldn't even man up for her. Me.

Time to move, now. I go out the way I came in: slinking through the underbrush like a criminal.

Fast Mexican music gallops around us and waiters carry massive, steaming plates of enchiladas, fajitas, combo platters. Beth sucks her margarita through a purple straw, her large brown eyes assessing me. Pretty eyes. Do I want her? My mind says NO: too flighty, nothing in common, skinny for my taste. My penis is in charge tonight, though, and it says YES, in big blaring neon letters it proclaims that YES, TONIGHT'S THE NIGHT.

She sucks, I crunch chips. I think: one more drink and she's in the bag. So I order us two shots.

"Here's to a lovely woman," I say, meaning it, watching her lick salt off her wrist and down the tequila shot. Down my shot, bite the lime, smile at her like I believe in her ability to change the world.

Which I do, to be fair. Women have this in them. Men, not as much.

Women change, inspire, and create. Men just bomb it or sell it or fuck it.

Beth's lips wrap the straw like they're going to wrap my stiff cock later. Wrap and suck, wrap and suck, wrap and suck, wet rose lips tongue tips does she realize what it looks like and that when she does it, I can't hear what she's saying? All incoming information goes straight between my legs to feed my erection. I press on my cock under the table and feel it lunge at my hand, good and hard. She's thinking oh, he's got a nice butt, I wonder if he'll be a forever man, a steady provider, true and sweet. I'm thinking oh, I wonder how tight she is inside, how her breasts will taste, what she'll sound like when she comes on my cock.

To re-enter the conversation, I nod congenially to whatever she's talking about and say "Yeah. That's great." I haven't heard the past five minutes of her dialogue. I have no fucking idea what has been said.

She nods. "Anyway," she says. "I got off on a tangent. What do you feel like doing now?"

"Well, you mentioned you have records? I'd love to hear some vinyl." I say, letting my fingers brush her arm, feather-light, and holding her gaze. She responds by laying her hand on my arm and smiling. *And I'm in.*

ᾧᾧ

We never make it to the records.

I hold her waist as we walk to my truck. She turns her face up for a kiss. She looks suddenly small and vulnerable below me but when I bend to her, she is insistent, aggressive. I am just ravenous. Her breathing is ragged and she is making these soft mewling sounds. I realize she is just as needy as I am and I abandon all reserve, pressing her against the truck door with my body. No one to see us in this darkest corner of the parking lot. Her small hand rubs my cock and I hear myself moaning, feel her ass with my hands, pick her up by the rump. I sit her on the hood of my truck, not caring if I dent it, and unbutton her jacket. Tearing her blouse open, I free her breasts and lower mouth to nipple, sucking so thankfully I feel like crying. I lick her breasts all over, sampling curve, areola, soft ivory skin. She growls.

"In the truck," she says hoarsely, arching herself against me. We fumble our way into the big backseat and I lay down, unzipping my jeans and pulling my dick out.

"I love your cock," she says, hefting it, squeezing it, hell, *appreciating* it with her hand and eyes. With her praise it grows harder, if that's possible, harder and bolder, and I feel a glow all over. *She loves my cock she wants my cock she's going to take my cock!* In nothing flat her mouth devours me and she makes these happy sing-song noises as she jerks the shaft, pulling and sucking and teasing me until I can barely stand it. Then I stop her, moving her off with a wet POP. I get behind her, wetting her with my saliva, and ram my dick into her ass, and she's fucking wild for it, pounding herself against my thighs and fingering her clit and yowling and when I come it's like white lightening inside her, sizzling across the night.

☞☜

Um, actually, that never happened. That's just my crazy testosterone fantasy. What actually happened was this.

"Well, you mentioned you have records? I'd love to hear some vinyl." I say, letting my fingers brush her arm, feather-light, and holding her gaze. She responds by laying her hand on my arm and smiling. *And I'm in.*

Beth drives a late-model tan Camry, the most non-descript and maybe most common car in the world. I have a hell of a time following her back to her place, a condo in Roxbury near Harvard Medical School. The neighborhood is on the verge of being good but also has a lot of Puerto Ricans. I don't have anything against Puerto Ricans. But they can play their music real loud, and they have some gangs. Just saying.

I'm on her couch and a James Taylor record is on. Her place is what the magazines in the library would call shabby chic, a mixture of thrift-store hold-overs from college and some stuff maybe from Pier 1. Fair-trade shit. But it all works together somehow, the dark reds and spangles and Christmas lights and artfully-arranged junk from other countries. Beth comes out of the kitchen, holding two drinks in Mason jars with straws.

"Mojitos," she says, smiling and taking a sip from one. "I grew the mint myself on the back porch."

I'm deciding I like her more now. The mojito is perfect.

"This is great," I say, meaning it. I take in her cute little green top, light blue skirt, points of nipples showing (*did she take her bra off?*), eyes flashing. Beth lowers herself onto the couch across from me and makes a big show of being tired, swinging her legs into my lap with a sweet sigh, catlike, stretching her toes out and kneading my thighs with her feet.

Instead of launching straight into sex, though, we sip those mojitos and start having a *real conversation* and suddenly I'm telling her that I've had my heart broken and that I feel like a zero zilch loser who has been thrown out even by cherished friends and family and that I was jobless and now I have a job I hate and that I feel like I need to let her know what she's getting into. Which is code for: I like you and I'm scared you'll think I'm too fucked up to be around.

"No. No. You're beautiful," she says, coming up behind me to rub my shoulders, getting deep, softening me until I feel like maybe it could be true. *Didn't she hear me? I'm a nobody.*

But her hands say maybe I'm beautiful. Lovable.

She returns to the couch, turning her body to me. I hesitate. She says, "I need to kiss you, Jeremy."

So I lower my mouth to her and then we're kissing, sugary and tender. The kiss lasts a long time, the kind of kiss you have as a teenager in the back seat of a car: curious and searching, then greedy. She moans when I squeeze her breasts, moans louder when I lower my head and bite at her nipples through her shirt, hungry for them. I pull the shirt off and lick her until her chest is wet, moving back and forth between both breasts, then holding them together to suck both nipples at once.

This licking and sucking goes on for a while.

Beth moves into my lap, grinding herself against my erection and moaning and moving like I'm already fucking her, like she's already riding my cock. I poke my finger against her wet panties and then tease it under the elastic and slide it into her cunt. My finger feels heat. She cries out and says "Now, Jeremy."

I pick her up as if I'm carrying her over the threshold and say, "Bedroom." She points and I carry her, lay her on the bed where she props herself up on her elbows to watch me undress. My cock springs up comically as I lower my shorts. I'm proud to feel it so hard. We both smile. She scoots over to me, grabs my hips, and pushes my dick into her mouth fast with a nasty groan.

I think I'm in love. I thrust my hips forward to get more inside.

She keeps sucking, not wavering when I move against her. I want to come bad but I want to fuck her, too. I want to feel the inside of her cunt. I want to make her cry out in joy. I want it to keep going. I want her to make me believe again. In love. In myself.

So I lift her up and work her skirt down to get to the sweet spot. We lay together side by side, naked, coiled like snakes. Sweaty. Kissing. Shameless. I push my full length into her juicy pussy and she whimpers. Her tongue swirls in my mouth, her heat surrounding me.

I'd give anything to have this feeling every night. To wake up with her, fall asleep with her, to make love to her, to make her smile. To learn her like a map. Is it being with Beth that feels so good? Or being with anyone, at all? How will I ever know for real?

She's maneuvered herself on top and is riding me home, fingering her clit. When she comes, she yells my name.

There is a luminous spray of stars when I come, my eyes closed tight but then crashing open at the moment I climax, pulling out of her and drenching my own belly.

If that weren't special enough, we collapse together naked and after a few minutes, *start talking again*. Laying naked, talking late into the night, and later, making love a second time.

It's so amazing and so perfect that I decide not to see her again. The potential for pain is way too high.

Chapter Eight: *Jeremy*

Watched the clock all morning, cringing as the minutes passed like hours. The monotony of filing and emails brought me way down, down into a hole where I felt like there wasn't enough air. Watched the clock and then left work to get lunch around 12:30pm. In the truck I shed my tie so I could breathe, ran my hands over my face, and turned on the radio. "Hair of the Dog" by Nazareth blared out and I turned it up even louder, singing along like a motherfucker, like the son of a bitch being messed with in the song.

I filed into Hardee's with a couple and their four kids, all of them roly-poly with round faces and red cheeks. Not in a cute way. In an out-of-shape, too hard to walk across the goddamn parking lot way. The kids' tummies stuck out of faded t-shirts. I pitied them. Didn't kids play outside anymore? Or were they all so addicted to computers and smart phones that they didn't even know what a fucking jungle gym was? The mother's ass was so big you could have balanced a vase on her butt cheeks. And the man – well, let me just say it. He had bigger breasts than Beth. And how could he fuck with his pecker buried under that paunch?

The beef tasted like stale oil and my fries were limp, drowned in ketchup. Not the greasy taste treat

I was hoping for to take my mind off things. Beth. Her smile. Her hands on my shoulders. Her voice in my ear, whispering "Harder, Jeremy." She'd left a few voicemails, each one more dejected-sounding than the last, each one quieter, like she was gradually running out of steam. Why couldn't I just try it? What if we were good together?

Amy.

I was looking blankly out the window, absorbed in my super-sized Dr. Pepper when the ostrich walked up, right on the other side of the glass from the fat family. I put the soda down, alarmed, and looked around. People were eating, laughing, zoning out. No one got up, knocking over their drinks, pointing. No kids screamed in joy. No one said "Oh, shit, an ostrich!" It was all me.

Nazareth's guitar riff blazed back into my fevered thoughts. The ostrich was not breaking eye contact. She was daring me, the bitch. The anger tingled in my fingers and my head grew hot. Ready. Ready to take action. Fuck this, I'm READY.

And then I knew what I had to do to be free. To get my life back. To be able to have a relationship again. To feel like a goddamned man.

I had to kill the ostrich.

⭯⭮

"Do you know what a baby rabbit sounds like when it screams?" my nephew asked me. Caleb and I were in the woods. I told him I'd teach him about the bow and arrow – when really, I was practicing. Aiming straight for the ostrich's heart.

The tip of the arrow slices in and leaves only a silvery puff of feathers in its wake.

"Like some crazy, wild bird," I said, making sure the target was secure on the tree trunk. The red and white concentric circles vibrated in my brain and made me excited. I noticed my cock was stiff and thought about calling Beth. Even though she probably hated my ass by now.

Bet she'd still take my call, though.

"Yeah, man. Teeny, the neighbor's cat, brought this freakin' live baby bunny to our back porch last night. I heard this like insane screeching. At first I thought it was like a mole or gerbil or something, you know. But then she let it go and it hopped and I saw the ears." He finally took a breath. "I kind of wanted her to like, tear it up in front of me. Like a nature show on TV." He looked at me hard. "But I also couldn't stand what she was doing. It made me want to hurl. I hated it."

We walked back to where the truck was and I pulled out a quiver of arrows. I showed Caleb the basics – nocking the arrow, drawing his arm, anchoring himself. The release. And as we took turns, our arrows zinging out to the target with varying success, Caleb told me about a girl at school. And I suddenly thought of something I hadn't before.

"So Audrey is waiting for me next to my locker after Biology."

I wonder if the ostrich isn't a mental aberration but a message. A sign from above.

"I've always liked her. You should see her hair. She has this really soft-looking brown hair. Tons of it, all curly."

Does somebody, somewhere give a shit about me?

"We sat next to each other at lunch, like every day for a week. But then people started to say we were a couple. You know. Like putting shit on Facebook about how we should update our status to "about to get engaged" and shit."

What does it mean, then? And what happens if I kill the messenger?

"I kissed her at the mall. I saw my chance and I took it, man. We were behind the sunglasses display at the food court."

Nah. Get it together, Jeremy. God could be sending you an archangel or something. He doesn't have to send an ostrich. You're fucked in the head, dude.

But listen. I am trying to be a better man. Better person. I have another chance. My life is on the upswing. This is starting to feel crazy – this whole ostrich hunt.

"Her tongue was so soft. After like two seconds my, um, you know, dick was *so hard.* I was scared she'd feel it and think I was a total perv."

OK. OK. I get it. Kill the ostrich.
But what if I'm wrong?

"Do you think I'm a total perv, Uncle J? Uncle J?"

Chapter Nine: *Cherry*

Cherry was still sweet like her name. Fueled by her breakup, though, she'd acquired a noticeable hint of tartness, like the sour pucker of perfectly ripe mango.

Taking hits off the bong and rocking some Creedence Clearwater Revival, she and Becca had gone through her entire closet one Saturday afternoon. The goal? Ballast anything that was dumpy, frumpy, or made Cherry feel anything less than beautiful. Meaning, much of her wardrobe got donated. They had to shop for new things.

Red liked her new things. Because her fantasies became more detailed, became weekends of desire luxuriating in her solitude, her privacy, strolling the house naked and crying out in climax as loud as she fucking well pleased.

Alone, Cherry was able to think about what she really wanted – not just in bed but in life.

And her coworkers were responding, too. One Monday, she breezed into the bank wearing one of the new things, a dark pink wrap dress with a v-neck, a piece that showed she was a woman. *Business feminine.* Cherry wore the dress with a turquoise necklace and shiny heels that ended in a sexy point at the toe.

Make a point, she thought, looking down at her look-at-me shoes. She'd never dared to wear anything that really made her feel even the least bit sexy before.

Tim from the corporate office was walking by her desk. He'd started stopping to shoot the breeze whenever he was in town. The past few weeks, they'd been dancing. The primal mating dance. And the pink dress was an animal display. Tim draped himself in the door to her cubicle, laughing, making a show of himself while Cherry preened for him. She felt her breath quicken and watched him seem to grow…bigger.

I want to feel your naked body on top of mine.

"Cherry? Would you like me to go down on you Friday? We could try this new position I read about," Tim said.

"What?" Cherry sputtered, shocked out of her reverie.

"Would you like to go out with me Friday? We could try this new restaurant I read about," Tim said, a winning smile on his face.

I wonder if he has a big cock. Cherry felt her neck and face flush scarlet with this thought and Tim smiled even bigger, leaning in towards her.

"Sure. Yeah. Yes. I would love to," Cherry said.

It was an Indian place. Tim made great conversation, always ready with a compliment or witty bon mot. He'd opened the door for her. He was attentive.

The curry was delicious. They laughed. Blah, blah, blah.

Cherry was ready. Wasn't he supposed to make a move?

Why do I feel turned on and nervous at the same time?

She moved closer, the smooth material of her green dress gliding in the booth, and put her hand on his thigh. She gave it a squeeze and licked her lips. A little trite, but it worked like a charm. His pupils dilated and he took a sharp breath.

"Want to go back to my room for a drink?" he said, voice husky, his leg tightening underneath her hand.

❧ ❦

The hotel room was beige, mauve, and ivory: a clean slate to write her passion upon. They were kissing as the door opened and still kissing as it closed. Tim kicked it shut with his foot, not taking his lips off Cherry for a second. Pressed against the door, she could feel his erection jutting out, incredibly hard. She moaned and his hand cupped her breast, pinched her nipple.

Cherry felt like a slut. Here at his hotel room, first date. She barely knew him. Her panties were wet. *Slut.*

"Do you want a drink?" he said around her tongue. "Mmm. I could call room service."

Her panties were wetter. "No. No drink. Just keep kissing me," she said. "Please."

The couch. He moaned as she traced his cock through the rough fabric of his jeans.

The floor. Her shirt was off and he was licking her breasts and rubbing the outside of her underwear. A finger slipped beneath the elastic and into her greedy slit.

The bed. Tim was gorgeous, lean and dark-skinned, with a thick cock. He'd undressed in the living room and left her dress on. Once they hit the mattress, tumbling through the fat white linens, he became much more aggressive, pulling her dress off and pinning her to the bed.

"Hey! Not so hard!" Cherry cried, his hands squeezing her breasts.

He growled, flipping her on top of him, taking her hips and grinding her against his dick, the head of it grazing her pussy. He smacked her ass and she yelped. "Still too hard," she said, on guard. Then he slipped inside her, no condom, no warning, fucking her like there was no tomorrow, his cock pounding into her, his face red and hungry and boorish, his hands holding her hips tight against him. She felt a bit scared – almost like she should tell him to stop, almost like she should worry.

Wasn't this what she wanted? A man who worked her over, took his full measure?

Despite the fear and shame she felt her body responding, riding him, her hands pressed down on his chest, chin and nipples pointing to God while her pussy spoke only to the wild stranger beneath her, inside her.

His brown eyes were guarded yet full of lust. They were fucking and yet, they were holding something back from each other – improbable secrets in all their nakedness. And when she came on top of him, it was that shadow secret that made her bliss feel forced, feel *less than.*

"You feel so good, Cherry," he said, moving her off. He rose to his knees and kissed her, then rubbed his cock between her breasts.

"I like *that,*" she said, wiggling her shoulders to move against his heat and stiffness. It felt like a massage to the heart. It was tender.

"I like that too," he said.

He took her from behind after that, riding her until he pulled out and came on her back.

Cherry didn't spend the night.

☙❧

She avoided Becca because she knew her friend would want to know everything. And Cherry needed time to figure it out, herself.

She was glad Tim had gone back to New York the day after their tryst.

Becca finally showed up at her door one night, carrying a pizza and a bottle of red wine. "I figured if I fed you, you'd see me," Becca said, taking in Cherry's sweatpants and puffy face. "You don't look like you've spent the week holed up in bed with your new paramour like I had hoped." They sat cross-legged on the floor, pizza box between them, eating silently.

Cherry took the last bite of a slice and washed it down with a gulp of wine. "No, I've been thinking," she finally said. She leaned down to grab another slice and as she pulled a string of errant mozzarella, Becca reached out to her cleavage.

"Ho, what's this?"

Cherry brought her hand to her chest, covering the small welt where Tim's mouth had been. "Yeah. A love bite."

"Is that a good sign?" Becca asked.

"I thought I wanted to um, get loved vigorously," Cherry said. "Get, um, *fucked* really hard," she said, spitting out what she had really wanted to say.

"Fucked. Hard." Becca's eyebrows went up. "You're preaching to the choir, sister."

"I had all these romantic notions of being swept off my feet by an amazing lover. Someone to break me out, you know, after Randy." Cherry's shoulders dropped. "But this guy turned out to be *too* vigorous. Rough."

Becca frowned and stopped chewing. "What do you mean by rough?"

"I mean, he hurt me. Grabbed me. Pawed me. And he *bit* me, as you can see."

"Are you saying that he forced himself on you?"

"*No.* No. I felt like running, though. You know? It was so unexpected. Like he was, I don't know, taking something out on me." Cherry looked down at the floor. "I feel so stupid. For trusting him. For going to his goddamn hotel room! For wanting sex so bad that I put up with it." She huffed loudly. "I always thought he'd have some kind of *panache* in bed. He always seemed smooth, sliding by my desk in his pinstripes and exuding this like, smooth jazz vibe or something."

Becca put down her slice of pizza and wiped her lips with a paper towel. "There's a difference between getting monkey-fucked and a good old fashioned ravishing, Cher. This guy was all monkey?"

"Gorilla," Cherry said.

"Asshole," said Becca.

"Shit," Cherry said.

"Shit," Becca agreed.

"I mean, there is a difference between how he touches my soft breast and how he jerks his fucking gearstick, right?"

"Or joystick," Becca laughed. "Or whatever. Why can't men get that? Don't just jump on top and *uh uh uh*, all ape-like, and expect the woman to like it. Did you even get any oral sex?" she asked.

"No," Cherry said.

"Well, shit."

"Yeah. Shit."

"Cherry. You know my position here: sex is healthy. It should only be as rough as you, the woman, want it. This is one less frog you have to kiss."

ॐ∽ॐ

She encountered Red that night, in her dreams, and when she opened her mouth to explain what had happened with Tim, he merely lay a finger against her lips and said "Shh. I know, baby. I know."

It was summer – hot, humid, smelling of flowers – and they lay naked under a tree on a blanket in the magic light of dusk. Cherry was flat on her back and Red was propped up on one arm, looking down at her. Golden dust motes swirled, twinkling in the air between them.

"He didn't know how to love you," Red said, running his fingers through her hair like a large comb. She purred.

"His touch was more intrusion than pleasure," Cherry said. "Not what I wanted at all."

"What did you *want* it to feel like, Cherry?" Red asked. He was tracing her collarbone with his finger, lightly but with definite intent. He followed the trail of his finger with his tongue and she moaned.

"Butterfly wings. Thousands of them, fluttering against my skin, iridescent."

"And here. On your neck. What do you want to feel here?" Red used the flat of his hand to caress her all the way from her neck to her nipples.

"The softest silk, tickling me to the tune of a string quartet."

"What about on your breasts? What can I give you here?"

She murmured as his mouth wrapped around her nipple. "Heat." She moaned. "The heat of the sun as it's coming up."

The tiny gossamer wings tickling and teasing, brushing over her. The silk, reminding her of both lust and innocence. Heat. And love. Red's hands and fingers roamed her, traversed her body and left intense pleasure in their wake. He rubbed his stiff cock against her thigh and thrust a finger into her cunt. He kissed her mouth passionately, then tongued her belly button until she began to laugh.

"What about here?" he asked, slithering his finger in and out of her. "What do you want to feel right…in…here?"

While he'd distracted her above, she'd gotten eager below. So now his cock pushed easily into her wetness. She inhaled as he penetrated her. He was so thick, and hard, and everything Cherry had ever wanted. In a cock or a man. They came together in a crescendo of moans as the sun dipped below the horizon and a diaphanous blue spilled across the trees. Violins played.

Huh. Well… she thought.

"Red?"

"Yes?"

Cherry sat up. "This is just too silly."

Red sat up. "Silly? What? The butterfly-wing fucking? The oozy satin loving at sundown?"

She smiled. "Yeah. It's like a damn romance novel. I don't need to be tickled with a feather until I come. I don't need your abs to ripple, your hair to fly, or for us to come together in a shower of stars as my tits pop out of a corset. I just don't want to be, uh, *manhandled.*"

"Monkey fucked," Red said.

"So you heard that."

"Yeah, I heard that."

"Try it again, Red."

"You got it, Cherry."

And when she blinked, the scene had changed.

She was on her bed, tied up on all fours. Hundreds of red candles, dripping wax, lit the room with flickering and ominous light. She was sweaty, her hair was tangled, and her cunt felt wet. Used. Exhilarated. She was surprised to feel a collar around her neck.

"Dirty girl," she heard Red say as he pushed a fat vibrator into her slit, obviously not the first time that night. "Look at you. Tied up. Begging for it." She moaned as he pushed faster, tickling her asshole with his finger as he fucked her with the toy.

"More," she groaned, wiggling her ass at him. She was so close. So greedy.

"Whore! *Did you forget what happens* when you talk back?" Cherry heard it before she felt it, a high whine followed by a horrid sting as he cracked a whip on her ass.

"OH!" she cried.

And he whipped her ass again, twice, to her scream of pain and surprise. "I don't want to hear any noise from you. Not unless I say so." She whimpered and was silent. Her ass smarted. And she was very, very turned on.

Red came out from behind her, wearing a spiked leather collar and leather briefs that had a cut-out for his cock, which stuck straight out through the hole. Cherry's eyes widened. She couldn't wait to feel him on her tongue. Even though he looked ridiculous in the leather get-up.

"You want this, don't you? You want to suck this cock?" He put his hands behind her head. Cherry groaned and opened her mouth to take it.

Red shook his head. "I say when. Ask me nice."

"Please."

"Please, *what?*"

"Please fuck my mouth," Cherry whispered.

"Fuck your mouth with what?"

"Please fuck my mouth with your huge, hard, glorious ROD!" Cherry cried.

So he did, thrusting it into the back of her throat. Her nose was filled with the scent of leather and of his skin. She curled her tongue and used it to push against the head of his cock as her lips wrapped the shaft. She wished her hands weren't bound so she could hold him as she worked. She was losing herself in the sweet agony of cocksucking, the feel of him growing harder...

"Ugh. This isn't it, either," Red said, pulling himself back. Cherry looked up, liquid dripping from her bottom lip to the bed. "This isn't the hard yet loving yet ravishing fuck you're looking for."

"It's not? What the hell, Red?"

Red took off his collar and untied her as he talked. "I know. You were really into sucking my cock. Fuck did it feel *delicious*. You should have seen how ripe and red and gorgeous your pussy looked after I used the vibrator on you for 30 minutes. Damn. And I hadn't even gotten to your ass yet."

"My ass? What were you going to do with that?"

"I think we need something where there's more full-body contact."

The scene switched and the action was immediate. She and Red were completely naked, fucking wildly, his cock shoved to the hilt in her hungry cunt, rolling through the waves of the ocean right at shore. He had her pinned to the sand, and the way his thick shaft caressed and ravaged her made her insane. His mouth was locked to hers and she could taste salt sex seaweed. Underneath her hands, his strong back. His wet hair. The feeling of their bodies wrapped together, as wet and slippery as fish. *So incredibly fucking hot.*

"Oh, oh Red, oh, oh, this is what it feels like this, this…" She thrashed in his arms, closed her eyes, and came. And came. A few moments later, he yelled out and she felt his come explode into her and then start to ooze out, mingling with the waves.

Fuck yeah.

Oh, fuck yeah.

When she opened her eyes again, they were seated at a small café in Vienna, a haze of cigarette smoke around them. Both she and Red wore trendy glasses and black turtlenecks. There were newspapers on the table between them. He was stirring cream into a cup of coffee. It was an abrupt, almost painful departure.

He reached into his pocket and handed something to her. A shell, still wet and gritty.

"*Noch eine Tasse?*" Red asked, offering Cherry the cup.

They sat, legs crossed primly, in their turtle-necks, sipping their coffees as Mozart played in the background.

"Did we reach the state of nirvana you were looking for, sweet Cherry? Did I hit the proverbial spot?"

"You hit the spot alright," she said, taking a measured, rational bite of *Sachertorte.*

"So glad that I was able to please you," he said, winking.

"Red."

"Yes, Cherry."

"I love fucking. I love it. I love your cock buried deep in my cunt. I love sex. Man, woman, union. End of story. As simple as that. Fucking."

"Huh," said Red, taking a measured and much less rational bite of *Sachertorte,* a blob of chocolatey goodness falling from his lips to plate as he took in her words.

"But do we need all the porn? The smut? The romance? The games? The poetry? The drama? What about just having sex?"

"Vee must verk on this next time, Fraulein. Your time is up."

And Cherry woke up, alone in her bed in her pink pajamas.

Chapter Ten: *Jeremy*

The time was now. Nothing left to cling to. Nothing left to prove. Nothing stood between us.

It was just me and the ostrich.

There she was: gray feathers under a tree. My upper back cried out as I pulled the arrow tight against the string. My heart was rampaging but my breath was steady. Once I killed the ostrich, everything was going to be alright. I closed my eyes for a split second, saw brilliant yellow, saw the red and white circles of a target, saw my own face looking at me, slowly coalescing into a vision of the tall, beautiful bird.

There she was, shining at me through the dark. I let the arrow fly.

Oh shit! Wait! She's all I ever was she's all I am she's ME I don't know who I am all I know is that I am so lonely I want to die right here and right now and my whole life is worthless and always has been and oh wait I am wonderful and my life is sweet and always has been and I am tired of the way that people hurt each other and the war and the greed and banks and the politics the unfettered ugly violence and I want someone to touch my skin and I want Beth to kiss me because she saw me, really saw me, and I want to feel my cock inside something warm and I want to be a part of something good and I am angry at the way they've taken it away from me and away from everyone how can they do this how can they do this how can they? How can I?

When the arrow pierced her heart, she shattered into a million pieces, shards flying as if from busted stained glass, violet and ochre and green and pink. My chest constricted in horror. I dropped the bow next to my truck, ran to the spot where the ostrich had stood and saw the arrow lodged in the trunk of a tree.

Saw that I was standing in Amy's front yard.

Saw her shadow moving in the window, heading for the door.

I tried to pull the arrow out but it held fast.

Then I was running. I ran back to the truck, threw the bow in back, and pulled out of there fast, the tires screeching like they do in the movies, spinning in a fury of smoke and escape.

৵৻

I think I may have blacked out or something, because I can't even remember how I got where I got and how the next thing happened, really.

৵৻

When I came to she was in the chair, trembling, cheeks flushed, her eyes screaming *amazement* and *lust,* her eyes on my erection. *I'm going to fuck your mouth now,* I told her. *Open wide.* I drew her face into my crotch, fingers tangled in her hair like roots in soil, and fed my cock between her lips. At first, she bucked away, whimpered, sounded like she was choking and I had to hold her to my dick. Then the tip of her tongue licked at my balls once, twice. I felt her give, the lightest scrape of teeth, the moaning sliding slippery apricot heat of her. Braver, she increased her suction, her tempo, her hand wrapping my shaft and pushing mine away as she explored and took over. Quickly she lost herself: the good girl, the girl who was scared, the girl who didn't really do things like this that much, the girl who was closed, the girl who had been hurt before. And she suckled, became hungry, became wild and new, panting around my dick, her eyes surprised and wondrous with her own power, her power over me, reaching her hand between her own legs. When she came, her orgasm vibrated into my body through the very root and I was awed. I moved her aside, hearing her long and tremulous wails, not knowing if she was in joyful ecstasy or pain, not knowing what was to come, or if I'd ever see her again, or if I'd die right after this moment, because I was tilting her haunches upwards, plowing my cock fully into her juicy cunt, and coming and coming oceans inside her. She keened like an animal.

Like an ostrich.

Chapter Eleven: *Cherry*

Cherry and Becca were at the bar.

Stevie Nicks was telling Tom Petty to stop dragging her heart around.

Cherry had been laid off from the bank. A relief, to tell the truth. She'd finally got a job working in a bookstore owned by a lesbian couple, after searching for months. She let Becca dye a strand of her hair purple. She moved into a cheap apartment. She started wearing tight, colorful clothes she bought at Goodwill. She was no longer so pulled together. And she got her tongue pierced. She was dating – no one serious – and experimenting with her sexuality.

Red still came to visit, just not as much. Her dance card was full.

Another song, about man and woman as magnet and steel.

"Fuck that," Becca said, taking an aggressive sip of wine. She pulled at her orange leather skirt, which she'd accented with some leopard-spot tights. She spied a tiny hole to the side of her knee and frowned. "You are the magnet, I am the steel. More like: you are the gasoline, I am the match."

Cherry chimed in. "You are the frying pan, I am the fire."

"You are the tornado, I am the trailer park."

They laughed. Becca was seeing a woman now – Bronwyn, another librarian. Bronwyn had eclectic tastes. She liked classic literature, Guinness, belly-dancing, Greek food. And being submissive in the bedroom.

The gay bartender in black brought a bottle of Pinot Gris and filled both their glasses, along with a small pour for himself. "To bliss," he said.

"Any way we can get it," Becca said. They clinked. They sipped. They smiled.

Cherry carefully got off her stool, watching men watch her in her tight red dress, and went to the jukebox with a handful of quarters, determined to play something good. Her hips swiveled to the last notes of the song still playing.

The first quarter clinked into the machine. "Gonna Be a Heartache Tonight."

A big man was watching her, thinking nasty thoughts. Like, *Look at that little number, shaking her moneymaker.*

The second quarter went in.

By the jukebox in the banging red dress. All ass and mouth. Her, yeah. Her.

Third quarter. Cherry selected Don Henley's "All She Wants to Do is Dance."

She could be mine. All I'd have to do is take her. Preferably up against the wall of the bathroom at this bar. Preferably right the fuck now.

Fourth quarter. "Hey, Nineteen."

I'm making a move.

When Cherry got back to her seat at the bar, twisting her barstool to face Becca, a guy appeared. A big guy – all shoulders, solid thighs, strong jaw. Kind of nice-looking but with a dark, strange vibe about him.

"Buy you a drink?" he asked, putting his hand on her arm. Cherry shrunk back at his touch and Becca leaned forward reflexively. He reeked of strong liquor. Tequila, maybe.

"No, thanks, I'm good." She paused. "And you can take your hand off me, too."

His face tightened. He moved his hand and didn't seem pleased. "Sorry. Just trying to tell you how beautiful you are, Beautiful."

"Buzz off, asshole. We're taken," Becca said, angry.

"If you're taken, where are they? Your boyfriends?" he said. "Think you're so goddamned special." He paused, and his face got ugly. "Cunts. You know you want it."

Cherry turned around towards the bar, trying to ignore him.

He grabbed her roughly by the shoulder.

And as she turned to face him, and as Becca was shouting to the bartender to call the cops, a big fist entered her line of vision from stage left, making impact with the bully's jaw.

The drunk man collapsed into a red-faced heap at the foot of her barstool. The notes of one of her songs echoed in the background, along with the din of conversations. She inhaled to curb the dizziness.

The friendly fist belonged to a tall, broad man with blue eyes and curly blonde hair. She noticed he had a fancy arrow tattooed up the length of his forearm, encircled with dreamy-looking ostriches. It struck her as very odd.

"Thank you. It all happened so fast. He just started bothering me..." Cherry said. "Thank you." She shook his hand, the arrow arm.

He smiled. "You don't treat a lady like that. Not ever. Especially not when I'm around."

A dark-haired woman ran over to him, coming back from the corner where the bathrooms were. She was breathless with concern. "Jeremy – hey. What happened?"

He leaned forward and kissed her cheek.

"Just had to put an angry man down, Beth." he said.

Chapter Twelve: *Becca*

Her fingers flew furiously to capture the last words, the tail end of the story unspooling in front of her. It wasn't ending like she'd expected. It felt unfinished, flawed. There were open questions. Things left unsaid. Characters who never reached their full potential. Extra juicy love scenes she'd wanted to include.

But then, that always was the way. She'd create her beloved characters, give them life, put them in basic situations, and then watch as they fucked up, took detours, went crazy, and did things she didn't know how to explain.

She'd always thought that Jeremy would go batshit and blow someone's head off. In fact, she'd planned for Jeremy to take out Randy. And she imagined that Cherry would end up with Jeremy, caught in some dangerous circumstance, blinded by lust.

Blinded by the gorgeous, paper-thin connection between sex and anger.

"The. End," she announced, poking the period key with her index finger and snapping her hand back. She took a sip of ice-cold sake – the expensive kind, the only kind she ever drank – and smiled.

Red came up behind her. His arms wrapped around her, holding her softly against the chair. "So, who's the hero in this one, babe?"

Her mind flashed through the pages she'd written. She saw anger, beauty, hopelessness, ruin, turmoil, love, hate, sex, sweetness, surrender. Redemption.

Becca turned around, lifting her face for a kiss. "You are, baby. You're always the hero."

Chapter Thirteen: *Cherry*

Cherry almost took a fall.

Becca bent to see what Cherry had slipped on. "What do you make of this?" Becca asked, holding out a cocktail napkin. "Creepy, huh?" Written on the napkin in forceful, raging lettering was:

I HAVE BEEN ANGRY

ALL MY LIFE

I AM

GONE

"Shit, I think it means it's time to call it a night," Cherry said.

The End.

Made in the USA
Charleston, SC
16 August 2012